Adapted by Dave Lewman

Based on the teleplays
"The Curse of Savanti Romero" by Peter Di Cicco,
"The Crypt of Dracula" by John Shirley,
"The Frankenstein Experiment" by Brandon Auman, and
"Monsters Among Us!" by Kevin Burke and Chris "Doc" Wyatt

Illustrated by Patrick Spaziante

© 2017 Viacom International Inc. and Viacom Overseas Holdings C.V. All rights reserved.
Published in the United States by Golden Books, an imprint of Random House Children's Books,
a division of Penguin Random House LLC, 1745 Broadway, New York, NY 10019, and in Canada by
Penguin Random House Canada Limited, Toronto. Golden Books, A Golden Book, A Big Golden Book,
the G colophon, and the distinctive gold spine are registered trademarks of
Penguin Random House LLC. Nickelodeon, Teenage Mutant Ninja Turtles, and all related titles,
logos, and characters are trademarks of Viacom International Inc. and
Viacom Overseas Holdings C.V. Based on characters created by Peter Laird and Kevin Eastman.
randomhousekids.com
ISBN 978-1-5247-1670-7
Printed in the United States of America
10 9 8 7 6 5 4 3 2 1

 A GOLDEN BOOK · NEW YORK

It was Halloween, the only night of the year when the Teenage Mutant Ninja Turtles could walk the streets of New York City without everyone thinking they were freaks. But there was no time for trick-or-treating, because a Time Master named Renet needed the Turtles' help!

Together they'd chased the evil villain Savanti through time portals, jumping from ancient Egypt to medieval Transylvania to nineteenth-century Bavaria.

Along the way, Savanti had gathered a terrifying army of monsters, including the Mummy, Dracula, Frankenstein, and the Werewolf.

Even worse, Raphael had been bitten by a vampire,
turning *him* into a vampire.
Things were looking very, very bad!

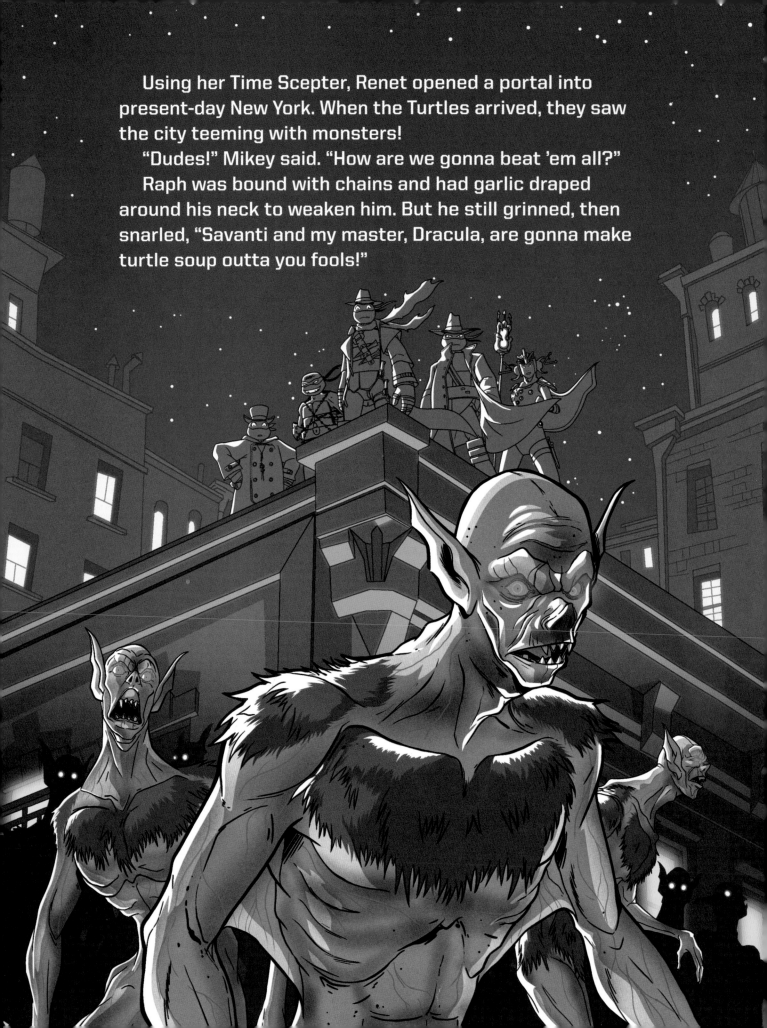

Using her Time Scepter, Renet opened a portal into present-day New York. When the Turtles arrived, they saw the city teeming with monsters!

"Dudes!" Mikey said. "How are we gonna beat 'em all?"

Raph was bound with chains and had garlic draped around his neck to weaken him. But he still grinned, then snarled, "Savanti and my master, Dracula, are gonna make turtle soup outta you fools!"

Raph screeched, summoning monsters to help him escape. A dark mist formed, and a cloud of bats flew straight at the Turtles!

"At least they're only bats," Mikey said. But then vampires stepped out of the mist, and werewolves climbed over the edge of the roof.

"There are too many!" Leo cried. *"Move!"*

The Turtles and Renet jumped off the roof, taking Raph with them.

As they ran through an alley, werewolves chased them!

Mikey tried to calm the werewolves with his beatboxing, but they just kept coming.

"Mikey!" Leo shouted. "Not every problem can be solved with beatboxing!"

Renet opened a sewer grate with her Time Scepter. The Turtles dove in.

Once they were all inside the sewer, Renet blasted the grate, melting it shut behind them. The werewolves howled!

"Home, sweet sewer," Mikey sighed happily as they down the long tunnel to the Turtles' lair.

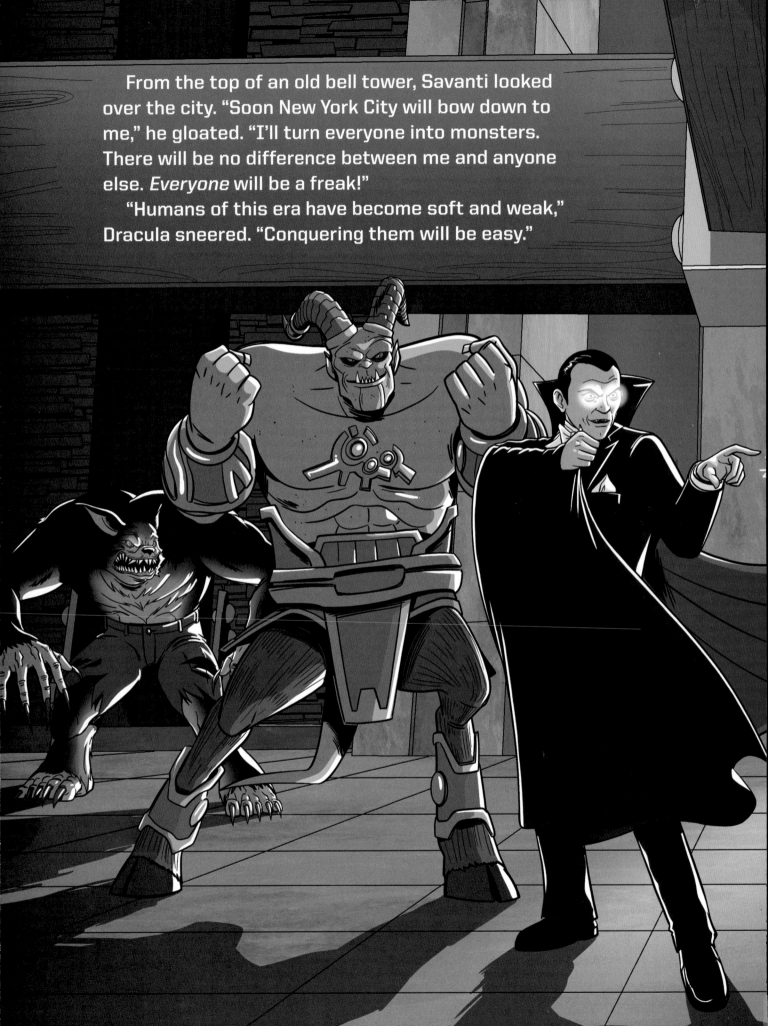

From the top of an old bell tower, Savanti looked over the city. "Soon New York City will bow down to me," he gloated. "I'll turn everyone into monsters. There will be no difference between me and anyone else. *Everyone* will be a freak!"

"Humans of this era have become soft and weak," Dracula sneered. "Conquering them will be easy."

Savanti wasn't so sure. "I still don't know where to find the Turtles' secret lair," he said.

"I do," Dracula boasted. "For I know the thoughts of every vampire ever bitten." He gestured, and April and Casey stepped forward. They were vampires, too!

"What is your bidding, Master?" April asked.

"Yeah," Casey added. "Whose blood do you want us to suck, yo?"

Down in the Turtles' lair, Donnie was attaching wires to Renet's Time Scepter. All their time traveling had drained its energy. "If I can focus the waveform, I can sync enough energy for a recharge," he muttered.

He connected a final wire. "This should put the scepter at fifty-percent power!" Donnie threw a switch. With a crackle, the scepter started to recharge.

Meanwhile, Mikey searched through old horror comics for the secret to conquering vampires. "All these comics agree—slay the master. If we destroy Dracula, every vampire transforms back into a human."

Across the room, Raph stared at Mikey hypnotically. "Mikey . . . Mikey . . . take this garlic off me."

In a trance, Mikey crossed the room and took the garland of garlic from around Raph's neck. . . .

The moment the garlic was off, Raph regained his strength! He snapped the chains, snatched the Time Scepter, and sprinted out of the room.

Leo, Donnie, and Mikey were about to chase after him, but April and Casey stepped into the lair.

"Our master has sent a message," April said in her vampire voice.

"He says *there's no escape*!" Casey growled as monsters filled the room.

"You're *mine*, Donnie!" April hissed as she jumped on him and bit his neck. *Chomp!*

Donnie pushed April off, but he immediately felt woozy and passed out, tossing his *bo* staff into the air. Mikey caught the staff and stood over Donnie, defending him against the monsters. "Get back, Evil Casey!" he shouted. "I'm *serious*!"

Mikey fought the monsters with his *nunchaku* and Donnie's *bo* staff. Leo ran up Frankenstein's chest and flipped out of his reach. Renet blasted away with her Energy Knuckles. "This is what happens when you mess with Junior Assistant Time Masters!" she shouted.

"Everything about her is the coolest thing ever," Mikey sighed.

Donnie regained consciousness and struggled to his feet. "Follow me!" He led them into the sewer and closed the metal grate, sealing the monsters inside the lair.

Meanwhile, Raph brought the Time Scepter to the old bell tower. But when Savanti reached for it, Raph handed the scepter to Dracula, his vampire master.

"With this Time Scepter," Dracula said, "I will go back in time to infect early humankind with vampirism. The whole world will be undead, and I will rule over it in darkness!"

"What?" Savanti protested. "No fair!"

But Dracula had no idea how the scepter worked. When he demanded that Savanti show him how to use it, Savanti laughed and commanded the Mummy to attack Dracula.

Smash! Dracula slammed the scepter right through the Mummy, reducing him to dust.

"Um . . . truce?" Savanti said, offering his hand to Dracula.

After escaping the monsters, Renet, Leo, Donnie, and Mikey had made their way through the sewer tunnels into the basement of an abandoned hospital. Donnie groaned and crumpled over.

"We have to stop his transformation," Renet said.

"And beat the monsters *and* get back your scepter," Leo added. "Our to-do list is full."

The Turtles dragged Donnie out of the hospital and pulled him into an herb shop to get some garlic, hoping to slow down his transformation into a vampire.

But when they turned to Donnie, ready to drape garlic around his neck, he'd already turned into a full vampire!

"Urrreeeshku!" he screeched.

Leo, Mikey, and Renet left the shop, only to find themselves surrounded by vampires, the Werewolf, and Frankenstein. "Good news is, this can't get much worse," Mikey said.

Then Savanti and Dracula arrived with Raph, April, and Casey.

"Okay, I was being sarcastic," Mikey said.

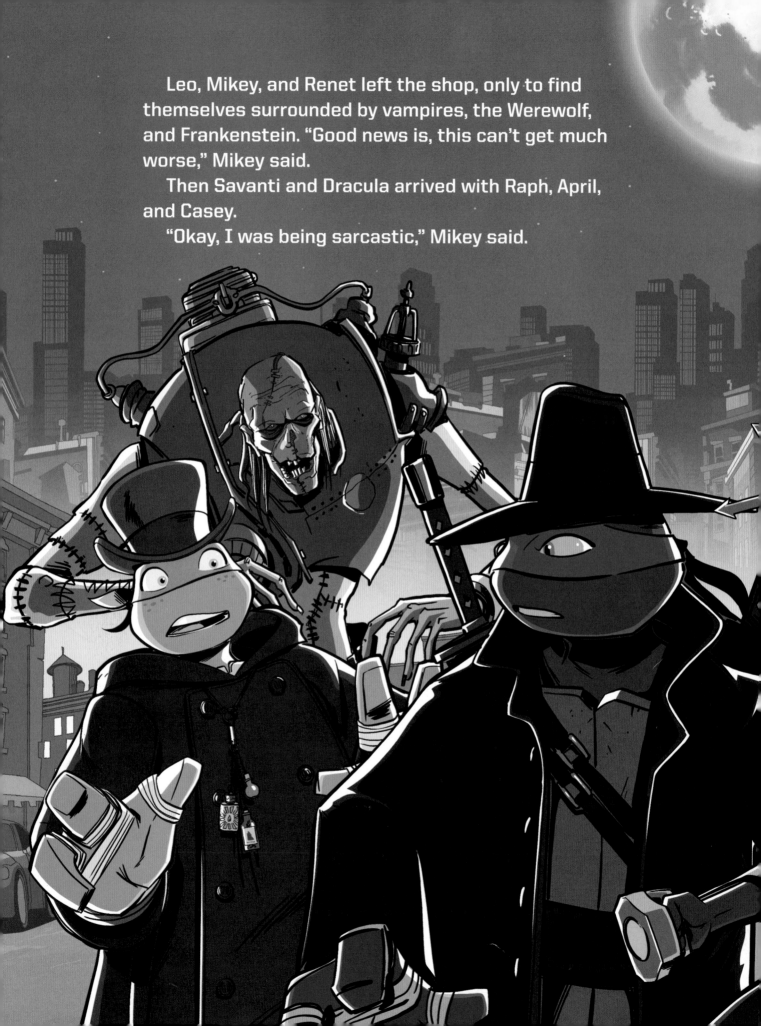

Renet spotted her Time Scepter in Dracula's hands. "My scepter!" she cried.

"Yes," Dracula said. "With this, I will make all of humankind into vampires. Monsters, eliminate the Turtles and the girl . . . *now*!"

Frankenstein lumbered toward them.

"Frank!" Mikey said. "Dracula is the *worst*! Does he even know your favorite food?"

The monster hesitated.

"I'm your *real* friend!" Mikey said. "And I know your favorite food is *frankfurters*!"

Hearing this, Frank shook off Dracula's mind control. "Mikey is real friend! You are *not*!" He turned and lumbered toward Dracula and Savanti.

They dodged Frank's attack. Then Dracula raised the Time Scepter, preparing to send the Turtles and Renet off to another time and place.

"The time is nigh for the utter destruction of—" Dracula began.

"*Oooof!*" Dracula grunted as Mikey pelted him with cloves of garlic.

"Suck garlic, dude!" Mikey yelled.

The Time Scepter flew out of Dracula's hand. Savanti snatched it and held it up. "Prepare to go to the *end of time*!" he told the Turtles.

Whap! Leo flung a chain around the scepter.

Leo yanked, sending the scepter flying. Everyone leapt for it.
Mikey whacked it with Donnie's *bo* staff, activating it!

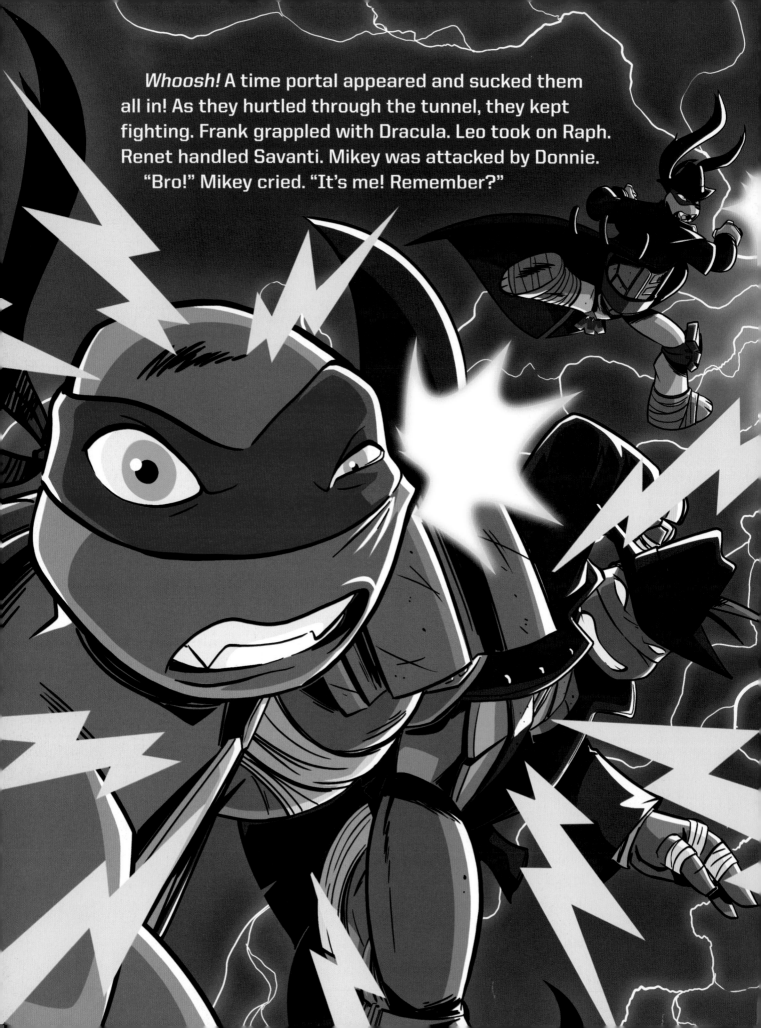

Whoosh! A time portal appeared and sucked them all in! As they hurtled through the tunnel, they kept fighting. Frank grappled with Dracula. Leo took on Raph. Renet handled Savanti. Mikey was attacked by Donnie. "Bro!" Mikey cried. "It's me! Remember?"

As everyone battled, the malfunctioning Time Scepter whisked them to the Middle Ages . . .

then to a dojo in the 1990s . . .

Amid the pyramids, Donnie got his hands on the scepter.
Renet spun and kicked him, sending the scepter flying right
into the hands of Savanti!
"Yes!" he cried triumphantly. "Travel back to where I belong!"
Whoosh!

The Time Scepter took them to the age of the dinosaurs! "Oh, not here," Savanti moaned. "Even ancient Egypt is better than this!"

As the others continued fighting, Savanti tried to fix the Time Scepter.

Renet cried, "Don't let Savanti repair my scepter! He'll be in complete control!"

Leo and Renet ran toward Savanti, but Mikey said,
"Guys! We take out the master, we free all the monsters!"
He stretched Donnie's *bo* staff toward Leo. "Stake me up!"
Leo used his *katana* blades to sharpen the staff. Mikey hid
it behind his back and yelled, "Yo! Vampire dude! Over here!"

Dracula roared and leapt at Mikey, who hurled the giant stake into the vampire's chest. *"Booyakasha!"* *Wham!* In a flash of light, Dracula turned to dust!

Savanti finished fixing the Time Scepter. "Now I will rule all of time and—"

Zap! Renet hit Savanti with her Energy Knuckles, knocking the scepter out of his hands and sending the villain flying!

"Enjoy the dinosaurs, Savanti!" Renet called.

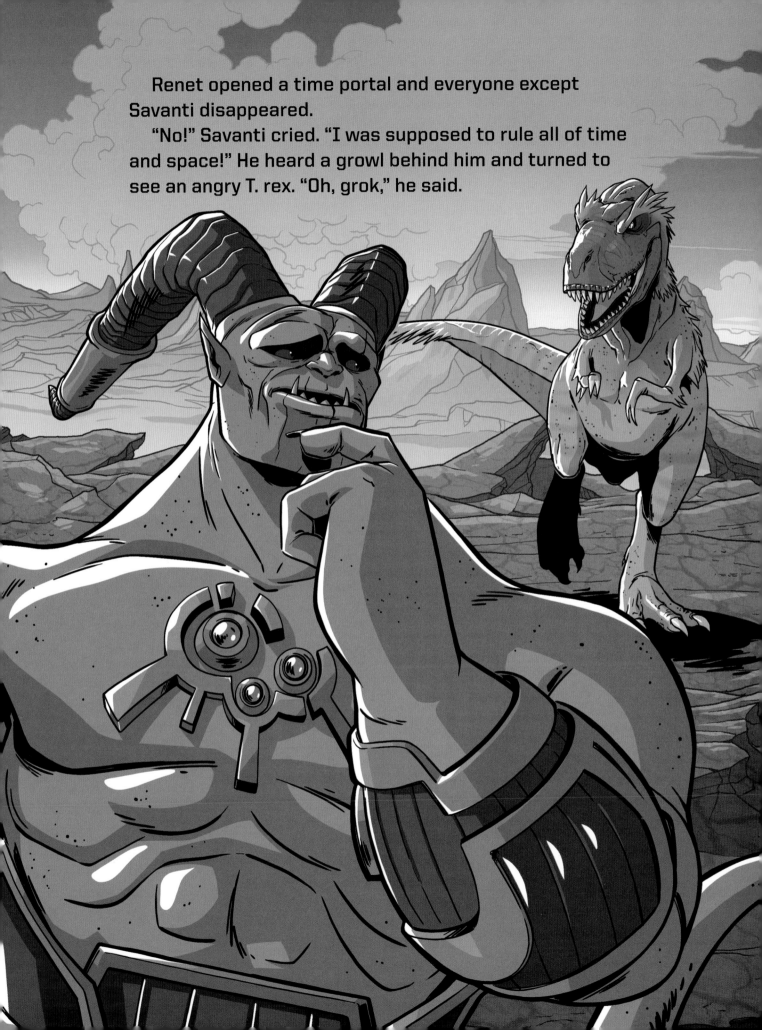

Renet opened a time portal and everyone except Savanti disappeared.

"No!" Savanti cried. "I was supposed to rule all of time and space!" He heard a growl behind him and turned to see an angry T. rex. "Oh, grok," he said.

In New York City, the vampires and werewolves had all turned back into normal humans.

A portal opened, dropping the Turtles, Renet, and Frank onto the street. Raph and Donnie celebrated not being vampires anymore.

"We're back to normal!" Donnie exclaimed. "Well, not *normal*..."

Renet told Frank she would take him to the future, where everyone would appreciate him. His eyes lit up as Renet opened another time portal.

Before she left, Renet turned to the Turtles.
"I can't thank you enough," she said.

"Renet," Mikey said, "you are the most incredible
person who has ever lived in the history of living."

Renet leaned over and kissed Mikey on the cheek
before stepping into the portal with Frank. In a flash,
they were gone.

"How about some trick-or-treating, team?"
Leo suggested. "The night is still young."

"*Halloween-akasha!*" Mikey shouted.